Hip and Hop

YOU CAN DO ANYTHING

WRITTEN BY
(Akala)

ILLUSTRATED BY
SAV AKYÜZ

OXFORD
UNIVERSITY PRESS

Great Clarendon Street, Oxford OX2 6DP

Oxford University Press is a department of the
University of Oxford.

Text copyright © Akala 2017

Illustrations copyright © Sav Akyüz 2017

The moral rights of the author and illustrator have been asserted

Database right Oxford University Press (maker)

First published 2017

All rights reserved.

British Library Cataloguing in Publication Data

Data available

ISBN: 978-0-19-274780-8 (paperback)
ISBN: 978-0-19-274781-5 (eBook)

1 3 5 7 9 10 8 6 4 2

Printed in China

If you're moving too fast, don't panic.
Use your brakes well, it's the best habit.

'Just slow down and take your time.
Practise hard and you'll be fine.'

'Kofi is right,' said Hip.

'You can do anything if you try,
You can do anything, ride or fly.
Don't let anybody tell you no.
Focus on your dreams and go!'

Here's Blueberry Hill – Hip and Hop's endz.
Where they go to school and play with friends.
Hop loves to dance. Hip loves to rhyme.
Come and join them. It's Hip and Hop time.

All the children are getting ready for the Blueberry Hill bike race.

Hip is riding FAAAAASSST!

The Cheeky Monkeys are doing AMAZING stunts.

Kofi is riding HIGH.

But where is Hop?

Hop is not having fun.
He dreams of racing his bike,
but he doesn't know how to ride.

'I don't think I can do it,' he says.

'You CAN do it,' says Hip.
'You have to follow your
dreams and practise.'

'You can do anything if you try,
You can do anything, ride or fly.
Don't let anybody tell you no.
Focus on your dreams and go!'

'Don't worry,' say the Cheeky Monkeys.
'You just have to learn to balance.'

'Riding a bike is all about balance.
Letting go of your fear is the greatest challenge.

Pedal and relax, let the bike do the rest.
Practise hard and you'll be the best.'

'The Cheeky Monkeys are right,' says Hip.

'You can do anything if you try,
You can do anything, ride or fly.
Don't let anybody tell you no.
Focus on your dreams and go!'

'Don't worry,' says Kofi. 'You just have to learn to use your brakes.'

Hop rides past Hip,

past the Cheeky Monkeys,

past Kofi,

and then . . . "HOP STOP!"

CRASH!

And before anyone
can say another word . . .

Hop flies off to sit in a tree.

'Little birds can't ride bikes,' he says.

'Little birds should stick to flying!'

'I'm going to tell you a story
about a little bird I once knew.'

'There was a little bird who was a trailblazer.
He learned so much that it would amaze ya.

He learned to write. He learned to talk.
He learned to fly before he could walk.

He inspires me because
he's smart and kind.
**The coolest bird you
could ever find.'**

'That little bird is you,' says Hip.
'You learned to do all of those amazing
things—and you can learn to ride, too.'

Hop practises . . .

and practises . . .

. . . and practises.

Soon it is the day of the Blueberry Hill bike race.
Everyone cheers as the children
ride past.

Hip is riding FAAAAASSST!

The Cheeky Monkeys are doing AMAZING stunts.

Kofi is riding HIGH · · ·

And a little bird comes riding too.

Past Hip,

past the Cheeky Monkeys,

past Kofi, and into first place!

Everyone cheers for Hop—
the little bird who never gives up!

And they all say together:

'You can do anything if you try.
You can do anything, ride or fly.
Don't let anybody tell you no.
Focus on your dreams and go!

Practise, practise and you'll be a winner.
Every expert starts as a beginner.
Drawing, dancing, or playing the drums,
With a whole lot of practice you'll be the one.

You can do anything if you try.
You can do anything, ride or fly.
Don't let anybody tell you no.
Focus on your dreams and go!'

WHAT DREAMS WILL YOU FOLLOW?